KU-386-016

QED Write On

Katie's Mum is a Mermaid

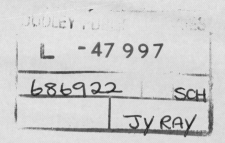
Copyright © QED Publishing 2005

First published in the UK in 2005 by
QED Publishing
A Quarto Group company
226 City Road
London EC1V 2TT
www.qed-publishing.co.uk

A Catalogue record for this book is available from the British Library.

ISBN 1 84538 181 5

Written by Hannah Ray
Designed by Alix Wood
Illustrated by Dawn Vince

Series Consultant Anne Faundez
Publisher Steve Evans
Creative Director Louise Morley
Editorial Manager Jean Coppendale

Printed and bound in China

Write On

Katie's Mum is a Mermaid

Hannah Ray

QED Publishing

There's a new girl in my class,
Her name is Katie Pew,
Her hair is shiny, all golden curls,
Her eyes are sparkly-blue.

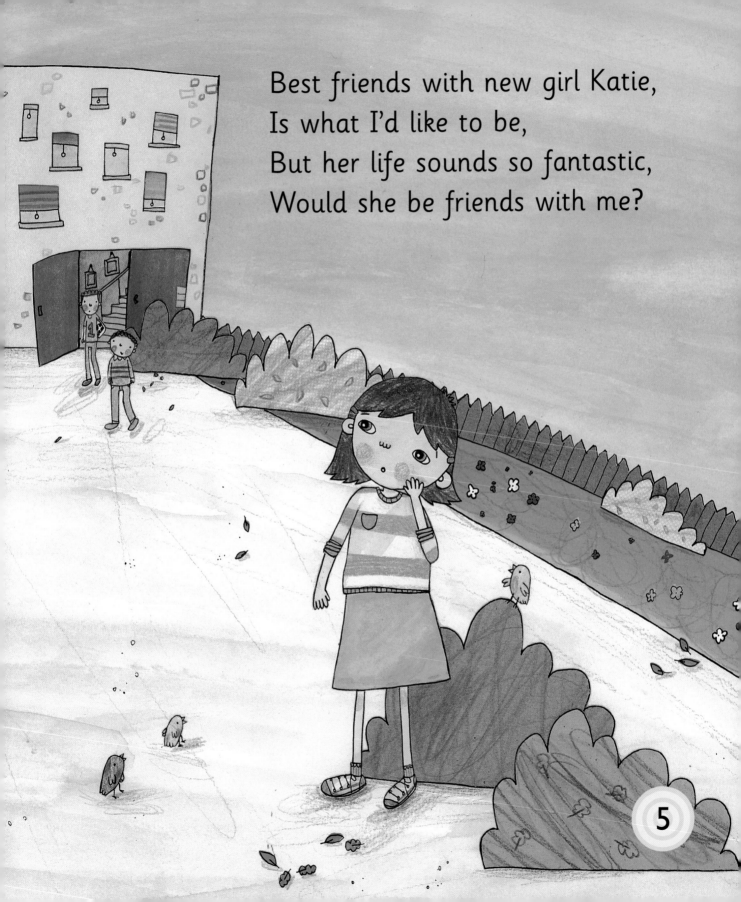

Best friends with new girl Katie,
Is what I'd like to be,
But her life sounds so fantastic,
Would she be friends with me?

She says her mum's a mermaid,
Who sings in an ocean band.
An octopus plays the drum kit,
You can hear him on dry land.

Her dad's a famous cowboy,
Who rides a big white horse.
He gallops through the wild, wild west,
Catching outlaws, of course!

7

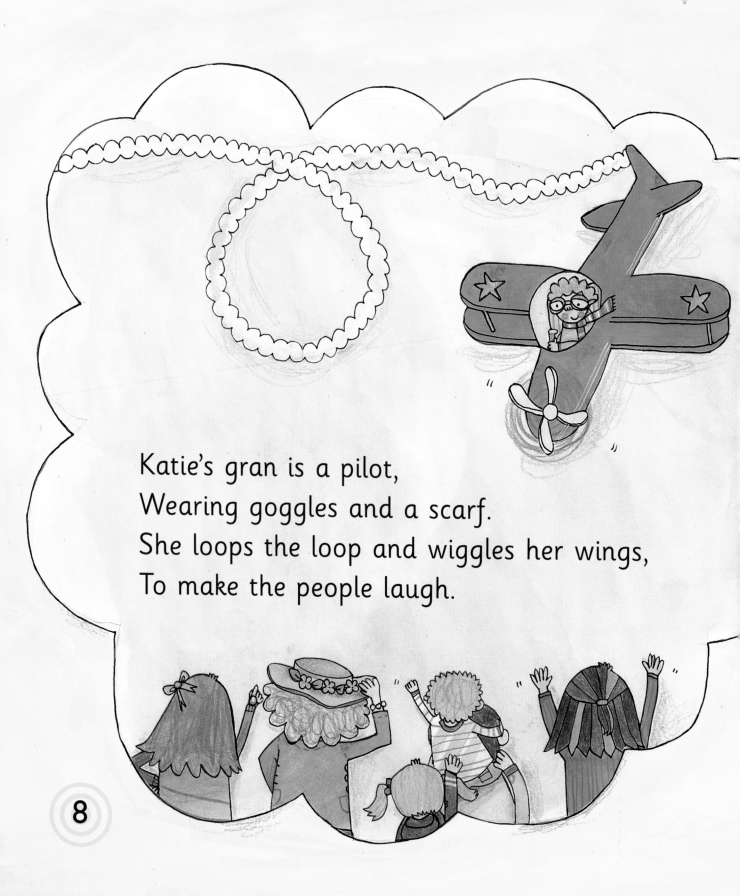

Katie's gran is a pilot,
Wearing goggles and a scarf.
She loops the loop and wiggles her wings,
To make the people laugh.

8

Her brother is a strongman,
Although he's only three,
Lifting elephants on one hand,
For all the world to see.

Katie's house is a castle,
With a drawbridge and a moat,
She says it gets quite chilly,
So she wears a giant coat.

There are butlers and a gardener,
A driver and a cook,
So grand it is, that Katie says,
The Queen came to take a look.

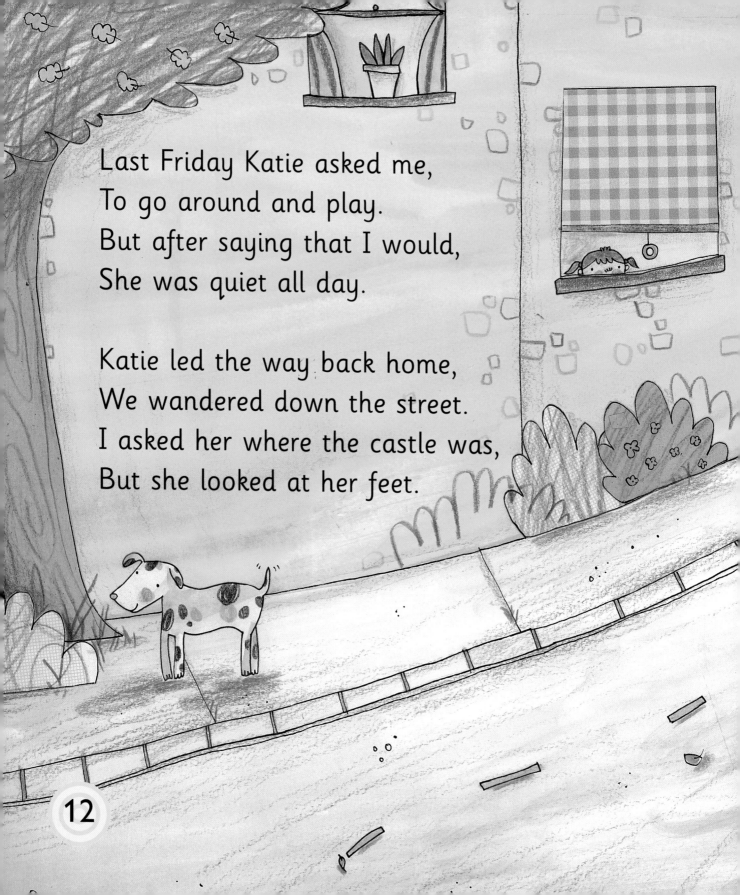

Last Friday Katie asked me,
To go around and play.
But after saying that I would,
She was quiet all day.

Katie led the way back home,
We wandered down the street.
I asked her where the castle was,
But she looked at her feet.

And when we got to Katie's house,
What a big shock I had!
A house like mine, with a bright red door,
Opened by Katie's dad.

A postman, not a cowboy,
Her dad delivers mail.
And Katie's mum, I soon found out,
Has legs and not a tail.

15

Katie's brother played with toys,
He showed me his best bear.
And her gran was just like my gran,
Though she did have bright pink hair!

But Katie still looked worried,
"I'm very sorry," she said.
She looked like she might start to cry,
Her face was very red.

17

Katie said, in a tiny voice,
"I told a fib or two,
But I wanted you to like me,
It's hard being brand new!"

But I am just like Katie,
I love to play pretend,
And now we are two princesses
And are the best of friends!

What do you think?

What words would you use
to describe Katie?

Can you remember
what Katie says
about her mum?

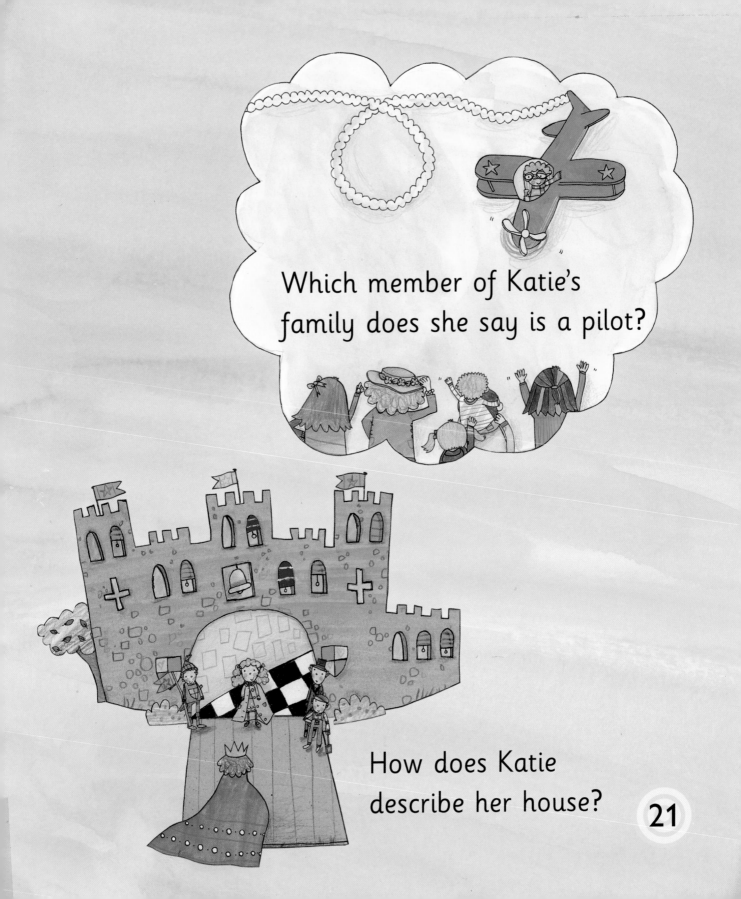

Which member of Katie's family does she say is a pilot?

How does Katie describe her house?

21

Was Katie's house really a castle? What did it look like?

Why do you think Katie is quiet once her friend has agreed to come and play?

Katie's dad wasn't really a cowboy. Can you remember what job he did?

Why did Katie make up stories about her family and her home?

23

Parents' and teachers' notes

- Look at the cover of the book and talk about the illustration. Read the title of the book. What does your child think the book will be about?

- Read through the book together but stop when you reach the end of page 13. Can your child guess what might happen next? Talk about the different things that might happen, and then read on to the end of the story.

- Look through the book and find words that rhyme, e.g. 'band' and 'land'. Help your child to think of other words that rhyme, for example, 'sand' and 'hand'. Once you have explored these words verbally, write all the rhyming words from the story on individual cards. Place the cards face up on the table and help your child to match up the rhyming pairs.

- Which is your child's favourite character in the book? Why?

- Talk about the thought bubbles in the illustrations. Why are some of the pictures in thought bubbles?

- How would your child feel if he or she were Katie's friend? Would he or she be cross that Katie made up stories?

- Encourage your child to talk about the members of his or her family. What do they look like? What jobs do they do? Does your child have any brothers or sisters? What do they like to do?

- Encourage your child to use his or her imagination to think of other things that different members of his or her family could do or be. Maybe a younger brother could be an astronaut? Or a grandparent could be a lion tamer?

- Remind your child of what he or she thought the book was going to be about, just from looking at the cover. How did the book differ from your child's expectations?

- Ask your child if he or she likes to play pretend (make believe). What games does he or she like to play?

- What is the name of your child's best friend? Can your child draw a picture of himself/herself with his or her best friend?